Ayah Hamad

authorHOUSE

AuthorHouse™ UK
1663 Liberty Drive
Bloomington, IN 47403 USA
www.authorhouse.co.uk
Phone: 0800.197.4150

© 2018 Ayah Hamad. All rights reserved.

No part of this book may be reproduced, stored in a retrieval system, or transmitted by any means without the written permission of the author.

Published by AuthorHouse 05/03/2018

ISBN: 978-1-5462-9051-3 (sc)
ISBN: 978-1-5462-9050-6 (hc)
ISBN: 978-1-5462-9049-0 (e)

Print information available on the last page.

Any people depicted in stock imagery provided by Getty Images are models, and such images are being used for illustrative purposes only. Certain stock imagery © Getty Images.

This book is printed on acid-free paper.

Because of the dynamic nature of the Internet, any web addresses or links contained in this book may have changed since publication and may no longer be valid. The views expressed in this work are solely those of the author and do not necessarily reflect the views of the publisher, and the publisher hereby disclaims any responsibility for them.

Introduction

- Sara is Suleyman Shah's only daughter. She has four brothers, and all of them are older than her.
  - Gündoğdu is the eldest one. He is 44 years old, born in 1182. He is married to Sude, a woman who is 38, born in 1188. They have one child named Ali, 3 years old, born in 1223.
  - Sungurtekin is the second eldest. He is 40 years old, born in 1186. He is married to Hateja, 32 years old, born in 1194. They have no children yet.
  - Ertuğrul, 36 years old, is the third child. He was born in 1190.
  - Dündar, the youngest male, is 16, born in 1210.
- Her Parents:
  - Suleyman Shah, her father, is the head (master) of her tribe, which is called Kayi. He is 64 years old, born in 1162.
  - Hayma Ana, her mother, is 61 years old, born in 1165.
- About Sara Herself:
  - Sara is 15, born in 1211.
  - She is respected by almost everyone, because of her high educated manners.
  - She loves fencing, hunting, horse riding and archery.
  - She is very close to her father.
  - Sara comes from Kayi (which means "the one who has might and power by relationship".) tribe.

Chapter One

Those temple guards! I can't believe that they caught me. My dad is going to get mad when he finds out. He told me not to go out of the tribe without informing him because he cares about me, and it's dangerous. But what could I have done? He was spending time with my mother, and I really didn't want to interrupt them. They were obviously having a private conversation because mom said earlier that she had to discuss with my dad something. So I decided to take a tour around the tribe on my horse. After all, since I don't have any enemies, no one would have something against me and stay out there waiting for a chance to kill me.

But when I was a bit far from the tribe, I saw about ten temple guards torturing and bullying a kid. I got so mad, and without realizing what I was doing, I threw a rock at one of them. I didn't regret throwing it at that guard's eye (my aim is really good) because he totally deserved it. But what I stupidly forgot to do was look around me to see if any temple guards were close enough to me to hinder my escape. I wouldn't have wanted to escape if I had some warriors with me. With three warriors I could have wiped them out so easily. Like I mean, come on! Ten guards bullying a kid. Wow!

When I noticed two temple guards running towards me, I quickly got my sword out. I easily defended myself, killing them. But by that time the other guards surrounded me. It was too late for me to do anything,

1

Ayah Hamad

and they caught me. I tried to escape by kicking the guard who caught me so hard on the shin that I'm sure he bled. But that didn't help. I was stuck. I had to find a way to escape. God help me.

I silently prayed, *Inshallah, I will find a way to escape without hurting myself or putting any of my loved ones in danger.*

When we reached the huge gray temple, they threw me into one of their many prison cells. God knows how many prisoners they have held in these dungeons. But one day, I know for sure, I'm going to get out of here and will take revenge for each and every one. But to do that, I needed to know exactly where the temple was located. The guards put something over my eyes when we were on our way here, so I couldn't see where we were going. So the plan was kind of impossible unless I came up with a way to find out my location.

After sitting in the cell, thinking of a way to escape, for a while, the guards pushed another girl into my cell. One of the guards looked at me and laughed "you're going to stay here until you die! After that, we will throw your body to the birds. They'll have an amazing meal!"

I smiled and replied "you guys don't have enough power to do that. I mean, you were ten guys on one little kid. And you're afraid I will find out where your dirty temple is. You know I will wipe you guys out of this world once and forever if I found out the location of this temple! And even when I throw your bodies to the birds, they will be way too disgusted to even get close to you. I bet you even the pigs you eat will be disgusted by you!"

"You'll never escape!" the guard cackled. The guard acted like he was going to come and hit me, but the other guard stopped him. "You know our master needs this dumb girl for some information. After that you can go ahead and kill her!"

Sara Hatun

They slammed the door shut before I could respond. Oh my god, they are messing with the wrong girl. I decided not to even open my mouth to tell them something, just to swear or spit at them.

After about an hour of swearing at them in my head, I looked at the girl who was thrown in with me. She seemed to be around twenty-five years old. I could tell from her face that she was having a hard time. When I was sure none of the temple guards were in earshot, I asked her for her name. She just looked at me and didn't respond. Obviously, she didn't know if she could trust me. So I introduced myself to her. "My name is Sara, 16 years old. I'm the daughter of Suleyman Shah, the master of the Kayi Tribe. You can trust me; I promise I'm not one of them."

She replied, "Nice to meet you Sara. My name is Halime. I've heard of your tribe from my uncle. It sounds like a really nice one. I just hope we have we will get out of here without any injuries or problems."

"Inshallah," I said. "Who is your uncle? Are you Turkish? Where do you come from?"

After talking with her for a while, I was so surprised. Her story was so sad. It turned out that she was a twenty-six year old (born in 1200) Seljuk princess. Her dad fought with the Seljuk sultan Alaa-aldin, and when her family (her mom passed away when she was seven, and she had a younger sister named Zeynep) left their palace in Konya, the temple guards caught them. They wanted Halime's dad to work with them against the sultan, his own brother! Even though her dad was in a massive fight with the sultan, there was no way her dad would betray his country for any reason.

So when he refused, they killed Halime's sister, Zeynep. They threatened to kill Halime, if he didn't agree to help them. But when he refused again, the temple guards thought they might be able to make Halime go against her uncle because she could easily marry someone and bear a Seljuk prince. After that she would have some power in the country.

Ayah Hamad

So they killed her father by poisoning his food. They lied to Halime by telling her that her uncle ordered one of his spies in the temple to kill her father to prevent her father from letting out any of the country's secrets or going against the country. But Halime wasn't dumb. She knew the truth and wanted to get revenge more than anything else.

I felt so bad for her and promised her, that I made her a very strong promise that I would never forget. "If I ever get out of here alive, I won't leave without you." I really meant it. But even though she smiled and u could tell that she really trusted me, I could also tell that deep inside, she felt we would never get out of here. And if we did, our dead bodies would be what gets out, not us.

But I couldn't blame her. She didn't know who Suleyman Shah was. I was sure that my dad would save us soon.

Chapter Two

Two days later, the same two ugly guards came into the prison cell. "Come with us Sara. Our mater wants to speak to you. Come on!" one said impatiently.

I didn't bother move. *If their master wants me, he will have to come to me. I'm not getting up except with force. I hope they will die. I hope their temple falls over them, and wipes them out of this world once and forever. Why are they such oppressors?*

But then the guard who wanted to kill me before (I think that his name was Tomas) pulled me up so hard, I was surprised my arm didn't break off. "If you give us a hard time, no one will stop me from killing you," he screamed at me.

I ignored him and turned to Halime "If I don't come back here and these bastards kill me, be sure that my family will save you. I love you!"

She looked at me all teary-eyed. I couldn't hear most of what she said because the guards took me away. But I heard her shout my name before the metal door shut.

That's when I got mad. I kicked Tomas so hard on his knee, and spat on the other guard. That's when Tomas got crazy. He took out his knife and held it to my neck. He was about to slice it open (I said the shahada, because I was sure that I was going to die. I wasn't a tiny bit

5

Ayah Hamad

scared. Because, just think about it! Dying as a martyr!) But guess what happened? The other guard (like he's my life saver or something) held Tomas's knife back and warned "Killing her would just end our lives Tomas. You know that our master needs her!"

"Yes Andrew, I know. If our master didn't need her, she would have been in her grave from the first time I saw her!"

Andrew didn't reply. He just sighed. I looked at him for a second, wondering why he was gentle with me. *Could it be possible that he's my dad's spy in the temple or something? And that he's going to save me?* I hoped so. I'd been in this dungeon for a couple of days, and that was more than enough. May God help me.

After walking for quite a long time, we reached their master's room. He was on his throne, waiting for us with a big, fat smile on his face. I looked around me and saw beautiful flowers everywhere. But there were lots of crosses and candles that totally ruined the scene. *Why won't the candles fall down and burn the place?* I wondered.

But their master interrupted my thoughts. "Welcome to my room Sara. I'm sure you will realize how sweet my temple is and not give me a hard time answering some questions.

I gave him a dirty look. "I'm sure that only the devil would agree to work with you guys! So don't bother waste your time with me!" (I couldn't believe that they were trying to make me go against my tribe and my own father!)

However, he just laughed and got up. He was so fat; I was surprised when the ground didn't crack. I wish that it did, because at least he would fall in it, and never see the sun again. He came up to me, and smiled "It's either you help us, or you get tortured so much: that you'll beg me to kill you. It's your choice. Choose wisely!"

Sara Hatun

I spat on his chubby face with disgust. He just froze there for a while. It was quite funny. Then he wiped the spit off his face with his dirty sleeve.

After swearing at me with some really bad swearwords, he slapped me so hard. And by hard I mean HARD! (Don't forget that his hand is fat!) I didn't cry though. I just glowered at him and was about to spit again. But sadly, I didn't have the chance to because he ordered Andrew and Tomas to take me away.

When we reached the dark and dirty prison cell, Andrew looked me in the eye and snarled "don't make our master Alfred angry again. You should thank god that he didn't cut your head off." And with that he slammed the door shut, locked it and stomped away.

Right after he finished his words, Halime ran up to me and hugged me so hard; I could barely breathe. "You have no idea of how happy I am! Thank god you came back." She beamed.

"Thank god," I smiled.

She eyed me up and down and then realized the mark on my face. "Oh my god, what happened to you? Did somebody slap you or something? They didn't harm you, right?" She fretted.

I sighed and glumly told her that it's okay. "But one day, I will return it to Alfred. I swear I will!" I was so angry; I could feel myself spitting as I said his name.

Halime put her hand on my shoulder to comfort me, and helped me sit down. I gave her a smile and thanked her. She's a really nice and trustworthy person. I wish that there were more people like her in this world. Because then, the world would be such a better place.

Chapter Three

Two days after my meeting with Alfred, on an early and cold Friday morning, Andrew came into the prison cell and flatly said "get up, both of you guys. Alfred wants you guys to go the cardinal. Who knows, he might be harsher than Alfred and convince you guys to give us some information we need."

Tomas came in after him and was like "get up guys, or else I'll make you get up by force! I really have no idea why you're making this hard for the both of us. You just give us some information and then go live the best of life, just like what all other normal people are doing."

Halime spat at Tomas' shoe with disgust and retorted "I'm sure that other normal people won't betray their families and country for some lame killers like you guys. I'd rather die than work with you killers or give you any information!"

"We don't help oppressors! It isn't only against our religion; it's against humanity, too!" I added.

Tomas smirked "I don't think that your dear loved ones actually care about you for you guys to defend them that much. I haven't seen any effort they've done to try and save you guys!"

Andrew sighed "for god's sake, just move. Let's get this stupid talk over with."

Sara Hatun

We didn't bother move, so Tomas harshly grabbed Halime's arm. I quickly got up and provoked "thank god our religion is against hurting women in any matter. Because that really shows if a male is a man or not!"

**

They tied our hands with thick ropes so that we won't try to escape.

I wondered who their cardinal was. *Was he as fat as Alfred, or as dumb as Tomas?* I hope that we have the chance to escape before it becomes too late.

When we got out of the temple, (Andrew, Tomas and about 13 warriors were with us) they gave us horses, because they said that the journey was going to be really long. If my hands weren't tied, I would have run over Tomas with the horse. He's so horrible and nasty.

About fifteen minutes after we started going, Andrew stopped everyone for a break. Halime and I sat together under the thick branches of a giant olive tree, and ate some food. (They gave us bread, cheese and water.) I really didn't want to eat from their food, but I had no choice. I was starving.

Sadly, there was no possible way we can escape. There were guards everywhere, and three of them were just watching us. They seemed like gigantic giants watching over their prey, making sure that it won't run away.

After about five minutes, Andrew and Tomas started shouting for everyone to get up for completing the journey. I was about to start running away when the three guards who were watching us went away, but Halime stopped me. "You don't know these people. If you try escaping they'll kill you right when they catch you. I'm not ready for losing you just like I've lost my father and Zeynep!"

9

Ayah Hamad

I smiled at her. "I wasn't thinking straight, thanks!"

Just as I got onto my horse's saddle, one of the guards near me was shot on his heart by an arrow. *AN ATTACK!*

I was so happy; I jumped up from excitement and fell off my horse. *My dad finally came to save me!*

Halime ran up to me and helped me get up. Tomas was literally so mad; you could see his face's veins sticking up. He was shouting "WHO EVER HE IS, WHERE EVER HE IS, GO FIND HIM! I'M GOING TO KILL HIM!" All of the guards were running around the place like little scared mice. It was quite funny.

I beamed at Halime "I told you that my dad will save us!" She hugged me and I saw her letting out a tear of happiness. "After months of being in that dungeon, the feeling of freedom is amazing!" she gushed.

After another three guards got shot and killed, my dad, brothers Ertuğrul, Gündoğdu and 6 warriors came into view. They ended up the rest of the warriors without any struggle (Tomas was so weak! Gündoğdu ended his life with literally one hit from his sword, without even dueling him!) But they left Andrew out!

I was curious for the reason; but I decided not to ask.

Right when I made sure that there were no guards alive, I ran up to my dad with a huge smile on my face and I hugged him hard for so long. When he said he couldn't breathe I laughed and let go of him. I missed him more than anything!

He held my hands and asked if I was okay, and I replied "as long as I see you, nothing can be wrong with me!" I hugged him again (lightly this time).

After I hugged Gündoğdu and Ertuğrul, I asked "Daddy, how did you know that they were taking me to the cardinal?"

Sara Hatun

He smiled and pointed at Andrew. "Oh my god! So Andrew was a spy working for you dad! I swear to god, I felt like he was!"

I smiled at Andrew and thanked him. "There's no need for you to thank me. I've only done my job. I'm sure that I'll prefer death over working with them!" We all laughed.

Then Gündoğdu pointed at Halime and asked "who's that girl?"

I called Halime over and explained to them everything. "Dad, can Halime please come to our tribe? She is a really kind hearted girl, and she helped me a lot!" I asked.

My dad replied with: "Of course, Sara. Halime, would you like to come live in our tribe, and become one of its many daughters?"

"I would love to" Halime answered with a smile. "You guys are really nice people, and I'm sure that I would be the happiest I can ever get with you guys!"

With those words said, we all got on our horses (Halime, Andrew and I used the horses that we came with from the temple, after ripping out the crosses from the saddle) and galloped off to the tribe, happier than we have ever been before. I really can't describe the happiness that I felt. Galloping off to the tribe with my dad and brothers, after everything I suffered. The feeling that you're finally with your loved ones and that all the pain is over. May god keep me always with my family.

Galloping into the tribe was the most amazing moment in my life so far. The drummers at the entrance were drumming their drums so hard, everyone was cheering and spreading the happy news. When we reached the presidency tent (my dad's tent), my mom, Sude (Gündoğdu's wife), Ali (Gündoğdu's son), Hateja (Sungurtekin's wife), Sungurtekin and Dündar (my brothers), were waiting for us.

11

Ayah Hamad

I ran up to mom, and she hugged me like she never wants to lose me again. I let out a tear; for I had missed my mom's sweet hugs, her words and tenderness. "You're okay, right? No one harmed you?" she worriedly asked.

"I'm aright, I promise. I'm sorry for going out without informing you guys or making any warriors come with me!"

"You made a mistake, but that doesn't really matter. What really matters is that you learn from it!" mom smiled.

After that I went up to Dündar, hugged him really hard and giggled "I can't believe that I actually missed you. Because believe it or not, you were the most person that I thought about in that prison cell. Our memories and fights changed my frown to a smile, and my tears of sadness to tears of happiness."

"It was the same thing here! But without the tears of course!" he smiled. We laughed and hugged again.

After hugging Hateja, Sungurtekin and Sude, I picked up Ali and tossed him up in the air. After I caught him, I hug squeezed him so hard; he was so tiny and cute! After putting him down I asked him "how was the tribe when I was gone?"

"Everyone was sad. But I told them not to worry because you're stronger than the guards who kidnapped you."

I laughed then called Halime over and introduced her to my mom and the rest. I could tell that my mom liked her, and I think that the others did too.

"From now on, this tribe is your home, and we are your family!" mom welcomed her.

Sara Hatun

"Thank you so much! I will never forget your kindness, and I want you to know that I will stay with you guys until my soul leaves my body. I will always try to be a very good daughter and Inshallah one day I will be able to repay your gesture."

"The last of your worries should be about returning any gesture. Nothing is better than taking an amazing friend as a sister or daughter. From now on, you're one of the many daughters of this tribe. Have fun and feel free!" I smiled.

After dressing up and taking a shower, I went to Halime. She was sitting down, fully dressed (she was so beautiful!) with tears falling down her cheeks. I hurried and sat down beside her. "What's wrong Halime? Did anyone hurt you by word or action?" I wondered.

"No, no, of course not. But I thought of my family. It would have been amazing if they were all here with me. I'd love it if we all lived here in peace and happiness." She sniffled.

I held her hands in a comforting way "your family passed away, god bless them with jannah. I know that it's a very hard thing, but really, the only thing that you can do now is to pray for them. Your family can't be replaced with anything, but think of us and treat us like your family now. We all love you, trust me we do."

"Thank you so much, Sara. Until now, throughout all of my life, I haven't felt as comfortable with anyone as I have felt with you. You're more than a sister to me." she wiped off her tears.

"You know what, Halime? I think that I know exactly what will make us both happy. Let me take you for a tribe tour. You'll get to know the tribe, and see how everything works out." I suggested.

"Of course, I would love to do that!"

Ayah Hamad

The tour was really fun. I showed her the carpet weaving factory and introduced her to the women working. "The carpets they weave are amazing! They are really talented!" she praised.

I smiled at her "they are talented. I work with them most days, and I see the hard work. My mom is in charge of this place. Sude, Hateja and I are her main helpers. You should be one of us too!"

After that I took her to the tribe's pasture. She loved the sheep, and especially the small tiny lambs. We played with them for a while, and then I took her to the horses' stables.

I showed her my horse (I've really missed it). Her name was Karaca, which means "it's almost black" and also it's a gazelle breed. Karaca (pronounced as Karaja) is white but has a black crest, tail and black hoofs. After I fed my horse, I showed her my family's horses.

The family member	Horse Gender	Horse's color	Horse's name and definition
My dad	Male	Brown and white	Batur (hero, brave)
My mom	Female	Brown and white	Prenses (princess)
Gündoğdu	Male	White	Bora (strong wind/storm)
Sungurtekin	Male	Brown	Burak (lightning)
Dündar	Male	White	Düldül (funny)
Ertuğrul	Male	White	Tulpar (A winged horse in Turkic mythology.)
Hateja	Female	Brown and white	Şirin (sweet, lovely)
Sude	Female	Black and white	Siyah (black)

Sara Hatun

After she met all of the horses, I took her to a stable that had many pretty horses. "These horses are owned by my dad. He wants you to choose one of them for you.

Halime immediately smiled, and after a short while, she chose a white horse, with blue eyes. It was really pretty. "I want you to name her, Sara!" she bubbled, turning to me.

I was pleased, and after a while of thinking, I suggested the name Aysun. (It means as beautiful as moon.)

"What a great name! I really like it. It's simple and really suits her!" She said while helping the horse get out of its stable and feeding it a carrot. It was already clean and had a full saddle kit on.

After a while of Halime playing around with the horse, we took the horse to my family's horse pasture. But before Halime put her horse in the stall next to Karaca's stall, she asked if we can go horse riding in the open fields outside the tribe. "I really miss racing the wind on a horse!" She exclaimed.

"Sure" I replied. "But this time, I will not go anywhere without asking my dad!"

We both laughed and headed off to my dad. (He was in the presidency tent with Sungurtekin.) "You can go out dear, but you have to take at least one warrior with you." My dad answered.

"But dad, I don't need a guard or something. I'm not a baby. Please dad, can we go out alone?" I begged.

"We will be good on our own, I promise." Halime added.

"No girls. You can choose between this and not going out at all!" he firmly said. I sighed.

Ayah Hamad

"Why don't you ask Mehmet (Andrew's real name) if he can join you?" Sungurtekin suggested.

"Great idea!" I smiled. Halime nodded. Mehmet was my favorite warrior. He saved my life more than once, so I actually trusted him.

After Mehmet agreed on joining us, we were all racing past the wind, our horses galloping into the huge green fields outside the tribe entrance. It was such a gorgeous feeling; spending time with Karaca after my long absence. I could tell that she was enjoying it too, because she was more hyper than usual. After a while, Mehmet stopped us and suggested a horse riding race.

I agreed right away, but Halime complained "Come on, guys! The race won't be fair! You guys are way better at riding than me!"

Mehmet sighed "so you think that you will lose, right?"

"Obviously" she replied.

"You haven't tried yet! Come on, you can do it!" I argued.

"Oof, okay! But if I lose, it'll be your fault!" She finally gave up.

So we all went to the starting line (A large tree) and after the count of three we galloped off as fast as bolts of lightning. We were all at the same speed, but Mehmet started becoming faster. So I kicked Karaca and she set off even faster. It was a hard race; Mehmet was a really talented horse rider. Logically, he won. I came second, but Halime was very close to me.

Mehmet smiled at us and concluded "you guys need more practice. We should start coming here more often!"

"Sure" I answered. "But don't keep your hopes too high. I'm sure that I'm going to beat you next time!"

Sara Hatun

"Yeah!" he answered with a laugh. "Come on, let's go. And here's some advice. You two should start eating more, because I really think that even paper is a fatter than you."

I glared at him "watch out Mehmet! You eat too much; I'm worried whether you'll start cracking the ground when you walk like Alfred!" (He wasn't fat; he had muscles) Halime burst out laughing.

As the wind was rushing past me, and as this huge small started forming on my face, I thanked god for everything. For the fact that I am still alive today and that I'm with my family once again. May god keep this blessing with me forever.

Chapter Four

"May I come inside Sara?" Mehmet asked from outside my tent. My tent is part of the presidency tent, but has a different entrance than the main entrance.

"Welcome inside!" I greeted as I let him in.

When I saw his face, I could tell that he was awake from quite a while, even though it was barley morning yet. I asked him curiously "why are you here so early?"

"Your dad was discussing with your siblings, some warriors and I something important. He wants you to join."

"What is he discussing?"

"Come and hear for yourself." He smiled.

I rolled my eyes and got up. I wondered what my dad wanted to do. He usually never invites me to these meetings because I'm too young.

"Good morning dad. Is everything all right?" I asked.

"Good morning sweetheart. I want to discuss with you some huge and special decision!"

Sara Hatun

"What is this really special thing, dad?!"

"I decided that it's just the right time to capture the temple, and bless it with the blessing of Islam. And I'm sure that you would love to join our discussions and help us plan!"

A wide smile spread on my face. "So you mean we will eliminate injustice, and help lots of people? And as well, we can take revenge for Halime's family!"

"Yes true, her family would be able to rest in peace. May god bless them with jannah." My dad replied.

"Amen!"

For the next couple days, the whole tribe was busy planning and preparing all different kind of things for the huge event.

Everybody was super excited and happy; especially Halime. She literally flew from happiness when I informed her. She was helping my dad too by giving him some information that Mehmet didn't know.

My dad planned to actually go capture the temple really soon; like after a day or two. It really depends on whether his plan works out or not.

So basically, he sent about ten worriers to the temple. My dad knew where a secret entrance to the temple was (Mehmet informed him about it) and the ten worriers entered from there. They acted like one of them was a prophet from the cardinal to Alfred; and that he had ten warriors with him to protect him. Their mission was to kill the guards at the secret entrance right before the group entering the temple arrives.

I was so excited; this was the first time I go to an actual battle. My dad though, just like our religion advices, asked the king of the temple if he would give up on the temple and hand it over without any war, but the king refused.

Ayah Hamad

He obviously doesn't know that we know about the secret entrance. But as long as our intention is clearly to Allah, and that we believe in spreading Islam and stopping injustice; god will support us and be by our side.

We will never force the people in the temple (other than the ones fighting us; for example the many innocent families living there) to change their religion or to move out of their homes.

Our point is to spread justice; and just like our religion says, turning any land into an Islamic land with kind words and actions is way better than capturing the land with battle.

After all, people in this world are free. God knew what they will commit in their lives before he created them. So, if they want to come into Islam, they are more than welcomed to. And if they disobey god but live with us in peace, then we treat them with fairness and kindness. What is between them and god, will stay between them and god. We do not harm anyone who didn't commit any harm us, but we are ready to eliminate people who are unfair and greedy for their personal needs.

Allah swt has said *"O you, who believe, stand firm for justice even against your own selves."* Surat An-nissa 4:135

The next day, my dad wanted a special dinner to be done, so I helped my mom and the other women make dinner. It was really boring, but I had to help them because there was a lot of work to be done. Halime was learning a lot of stuff; she hasn't proper cooked before.

When all of the family members gathered for dinner, we started eating. The dinner was fabulous, but I really wanted to know why dad wanted a special dinner today.

Finally after everyone had finished their first plate, my dad started speaking. "I decided that this calm night will be the night we head

Sara Hatun

off for capturing the temple. So right after we all pray Ishaa, I want everyone who's joining us to meet here, in this tent!"

Wow! I dropped my spoon onto the floor; for this was such a surprise! My brothers were happy too, but you can't have compared anyone's happiness with Halime's happiness.

I wasn't surprised, because like duh, they killed her father, sister and made her life miserable. After everyone got back to normal, she turned to my dad, "I really want to do something before you guys head off to the temple, if you kindly allow me to."

My dad replied with a kind and warm smile. "Go ahead and ask sweetheart!"

"If you're okay with it, I would love to go and visit my father's grave. I know where the temple guards buried him. I really want to read to him some Quran and make duaa."

"I will never disagree to something like this. Of course you can go, but you have to take some warriors with you. I'm sure that it will not be safe there."

"Can I go with her dad?" I pleaded.

"Dad, I can take them if you want. I'll have three of my warriors with me." Ertuğrul suggested.

"Okay!" my dad said, answering us all. "You guys set off after dinner, while we prepare some things for tonight."

Right after we finished dinner, Ertuğrul called his warriors over and we all set off on our horses.

As Halime lead us, we reached the area after a short period of time. It wasn't really far from the tribe.

Ayah Hamad

Halime quickly got off her horse and rushed to her father's grave. She made some duaa, read Quran and started crying. I went over to her and put my hand around her waist, and then she started crying on to my shoulder. Right when she wiped off her tears, we all heard a movement in the bushes.

"Ertuğrul, protect Halime, she doesn't have a sword!" I shouted over to Ertuğrul as I got up.

I quickly grabbed my sword out of its scabbard, and sure enough, ten temple guards appeared from behind the bushes. I had no idea how they knew that we were coming here, but it wasn't the right time to think about it.

"Hand us over Halime, and we will let you guys all go!" one of the guards called out in a disgusting and cruel voice.

"I'd rather give my life away than hand her over to you guys!" Ertuğrul fumed loudly.

I glimpsed Halime give Ertuğrul a cute and admiring look that made me smile. But I quickly got into action when one of the guards aimed his sword at me. We dueled for quite a long time, but I won him at the end.

Just as I turned to see if there were any guards behind me, I caught notice of a guard aiming with his bow at Halime. It all seemed to happen in slow motion.

I started yelling her name to warn her, and when I realized that the arrow was going out of the bow, I started to run towards her. I had a terrible and awful feeling that I was going to lose her now.

But just as the arrow was about to push into Halime's body, Ertuğrul sliced it into half.

Sara Hatun

He saved her life, how sweet! The two of them were coming a lot to my mind recently. They really suited each other! A gorgeous cute woman and a brave, strong and hot man. I'm not even exaggerating; they would make a perfect couple.

After the awful incident, Ertuğrul and his warriors easily finished up with the other warriors.

I was too worried and rushed over to Halime to make sure that she was okay. She was okay, thank god, but was worried. I calmed her down, gave her water and helped her get settled onto her horse's saddle.

Moments after, we were all on our way to the tribe. Right when we reached, Ertuğrul, his warriors and I rushed over to my dad, just as we agreed before we went out, so that we can discuss the plan. It was quite complicated, but sounded really exciting.

So, basically what was going to happen was that right after Ishaa, the ten warriors inside the temple will get rid of the knights that guard the secret entrance.

My dad divided us into two groups. Ertuğrul, Sungurtekin, Dündar and quite a big number of warriors would enter the temple from the secret entrance.

The other group which consists of my dad, Gündoğdu, a small amount of warriors and I would stay outside the temple and make sure that everything is right.

When Ertuğrul and the rest get into the temple, the secret pathway would lead them to the temple's prison. There they would free all of the slaves and prisoners.

While they are doing this, the ten warriors (supposedly the 'trader and his warriors' (after ending of the guards at the secret pathway)) would

23

Ayah Hamad

be keeping Alfred and his leaders busy in the main room by explaining their message from the cardinal and so on.

After Ertuğrul, Dündar and Sungurtekin take over the entire temple; they will go to the main room. There they will get rid of the criminal Alfred and his friends.

When everything is finished inside, Ertuğrul should climb on top of the temple's main door to a small area filled with huge crucifix flags that show visitors and arrivers that this is a temple. What he has to do to the flags is to throw them down to the ground by cutting them off with his magical sword. After that, he should raise the amazing Kayı flags up high to show that this isn't a temple anymore.

The warriors should open the main gate, and when our group outside sees that, we should join Ertuğrul, Dündar and Sungurtekin inside the temple. And with that, we would have captured the temple.

The plan sounds easy, but I know that that it will be very difficult. May god help us when we set off. Because I know that we will never succeed if god doesn't want us to.

Inshallah god will be by our side, and always help us select the right path.

Inshallah god will forbid us from selecting the wrong path.

Inshallah god will help us eliminate injustice before it overcomes the world.

Amen!

Chapter Five

"Allahu Akbar, Allahu Akbar, Allahu Akbar, Allahu Akbar!" The athan for Ishaa rose up from the center of the tribe. My dad decided on not praying in the mosque with the other men, but to pray with the whole family. He decided to do that because who knows; he might never come back from the temple attack. God bless him and make his life longer and longer. He's honestly the closest person to my heart.

When the whole family gathered, my dad started the prayer. He ended it with a powerful duaa: *"He who says: Be! And it is... And who filled our hearts with faith, with the 99 names of Allah the Almighty. Oh Allah, on the path of battle, clear the traps out of our way. Make us alert against the enemies. Oh Allah, give our sword the strength of Zülfikar... and give our heart the courage of the blessed Omar. Our brotherhood, our unity... don't give them the unity to destroy our subsistence. We ask only for your help, and we kneel only for you! Oh Allah, please be with us! Ya Allah, when we are away from the tribe, keep our woman and children safe. Amen!"*

"Amen!" we all said.

It was time to go! My dad hugged my mom and Ali goodbye, and my brothers and I did the same. After that I watched Sungurtekin and Gündoğdu hug their wives. I looked at Ertuğrul and Halime. It would've been sweet if they were married. *They really suite each other! I*

25

Ayah Hamad

think about this every time both of them are in the same place; I can't help it!

As we all headed out of the tribe, I was nervous and kind of scared. It was the first time that I ever attend something as serious as this, and I was worried whether I'll muck it all up. I hope not; or else I don't know how I would ever look at anyone's face again.

I'm over exaggerating; not like I have a big job anyways.

Mehmet lead us to the temple (it was well hidden), and we parked our horses quietly near a huge field of bushes. It was impossible for anyone to spot us because it was dark and we were surrounded by thick trees.

Dad went up to Ertuğrul, Sungurtekin and Dündar and hugged them one by one.

"May Allah be with you guys!" I smiled at them and watched as Mehmet called them over to lead them to the temple's secret entrance.

After that everyone else gathered around dad. "The time has come, and it's our turn now. Today we will stand against the oppressor and help the oppressed!"

"Allahu Akbar!"

"Come on, brave warriors! Everyone go ahead and take your position!" my dad divided us into two groups. The first group was led by him. It contained ten warriors and me.

The second group was led by Gündoğdu and he had fifteen warriors by his side.

"Gündoğdu, we will take care of the guards that are guarding the entrance of the temple while you guys go take care of the guards that

Sara Hatun

are guarding the sides of the temple. After that, we will meet here. God be by your side!" My dad explained to Gündoğdu and the others.

"May god be with you guys too!" Gündoğdu replied.

"Take care, brother!" I shouted at him as he went away.

"You too, sweetheart!"

As Gündoğdu's group quietly walked away, dad started moving towards the temple. I was really excited but nervous too. My dad noticed and squeezed my hands for support. I smiled at him, but I was still nervous.

When we reached the temple, we could hear the battle inside. There weren't many guards outside; I guess that half of them went inside when they found out about Ertuğrul and the rest.

So it was going to be really easy to get rid of the small amount outside. My dad moved first. He killed the guard right next to the door, and then the other warriors on our team started moving towards the other temple guards.

Just when I was about to join them, I noticed a guard behind my dad that was about to hit him on his head with a strong piece of wood.

I ran quickly towards the guard (thank god I was near my dad) and stabbed him on his back with my sharp dagger. I stabbed him again right under his neck, ending his life.

My dad thanked me and returned to his fighting position. I observed around me and realized that there wasn't any free temple guard I can fight. They were all fighting with one of our tribe's warriors, so I decided to just watch the battle.

After a really short while, the men finished their job. I immediately ran up to my dad and hugged him really hard. I didn't let go until one

Ayah Hamad

of the men came over to my dad "Thanks god sir, we don't have any injuries or martyrs!"

"Alhamdulillah, so we might as well go to our meeting place now!" dad smiled.

When we finally reached the meeting place, surprisingly, Gündoğdu and his group were already there. I expected them to arrive a while after us because they had more work to be done.

But they informed us that, just like us, there were barely any guards. So dad ordered a warrior to go to the temple and check out when Ertuğrul raises the flag.

While we were waiting for the warrior to come back with the good news (Inshallah), Gündoğdu started a conversation.

"Dad, what are you willing to do with the temple after we capture it?"

My dad answered with a tender voice "my dear son, we have come to Aleppo because the Mongols were attacking us from the four sides. When we were searching for a home, the king of Aleppo welcomed us with open hands. So I have decided to hand him over this temple as a thank you gift. This temple will give him more strength and power, and it'll be a sign for our forever lasting friendship!"

"You've made a great decision, dad!" Gündoğdu approved. I nodded with a smile. I barely remember anything from Anatolia, but I do remember the long and tiring way we took to arrive here.

**

After a short while the warrior who my father sent came back. "Sir, sir!" he was shouting at us cheerfully. "They did it! Ertuğrul is raising our flag and the gates are opened!"

Sara Hatun

My dad raised his hand up and shouted "Allahu Akbar! Come on, my brave men! To the temple!" he instructed and started running towards the horses.

We all went after him, jumped onto our horses and started galloping to the temple at very high speed.

As we entered the temple gates, Ertuğrul, Sungurtekin, Dündar and the rest of the warriors were raising their swords and cheerfully shouting "Allahu Akbar!" We joined them, for every single body was happy with the great victory.

After a while my dad raised his hand and the place got quite. "My great and brave warriors, today is a great day; for a piece of land was taken from the oppressor! We will not use this land for a bad cause; but we will use it to spread peace and love between people. My dear sons, we don't judge people for their religion or beliefs. What is between them and god will stay between them and god. Our job is to give advice! We haven't taken this temple because it's for non-Muslims - but we have taken it because it's owned by oppressors! Our religion orders us, even if the oppressors were Muslims, from our own blood and country, we should fight them! Islam is the religion of unity, fairness and peace. So if anyone acts against fairness, they will find ME in front of him!"

"Allahu Akbar!" everybody went wild.

"Sungurtekin and Gündoğdu, you guys stay in the temple with half of the warriors and sort everything out tonight. Ertuğrul, Dündar, Sara and the other half of the warriors will come back with me to the tribe. Tomorrow evening, I will come here with the other family members." dad instructed in the main room of the temple.

"When I come back here, I want you guys to call over all of the temple's families for a meeting in the great yard because I want to speak to them."

"Your command dad!" we all replied.

Ayah Hamad

After that, we all hugged Sungurtekin and Gündoğdu and left for the tribe. My mom, Halime, Hateja and Sude were all so happy with the news. They had supper ready for us, but I asked if I can go to my tent "I'm not really hungry, mom. If you and dad are okay with it, I want to go to my tent and rest."

**

When I got out of the presidency tent, Ertuğrul rushed after me, grabbed my arm and said that he wanted to discuss with me something important.

And that important thing was literally my wish come true!

So after welcoming him to my tent, he started off with "mom and dad spoke to me two days ago about marriage. They want me to get married soon. And you know I'm actually quite old – I'm supposed to have been married ages ago!"

"True. But do you have any woman in mind?"

"Well, I've thought of this for a really long time. I have no interest in the women in our tribe; none seem right. So I have thought of…"

"Who?" I queried.

"But you have to promise me something first."

I rolled my eyes. "What do you want?"

"You ask the woman what she thinks of me before informing her about my wish of marriage. But if she thinks of me negatively, you act like I don't want anything and forget about everything."

"Number one, why don't you ask mom to do this? She's way better than me. And second of all, who is this woman?" I questioned/

Sara Hatun

"You're way closer to Halime than mom is." Ertuğrul said. Then he realized that he let out Halime's name that easily and simpered.

"Halime?" I exclaimed. I wasn't expecting that coming.

"Why do you seem so surprised?"

"I'm more happy than surprised. Ill speak with her tomorrow, don't worry." I beamed.

"Do you think that she'll refuse me? Considering that she's a Seljuk princess; she might want a prince…"

I held his cold hands tenderly to comfort him, "Trust me bro, Halime doesn't care about princes, palaces and all of these things. And don't speak about princes because you're the hottest prince I've ever seen before. Halime treats our tribe like her true home and she treats us like we are her real family. She is such a sweet and beautiful woman, and has faced a lot of problems in her teen years. I'm sure that you will not be able to have a better wife! And I'm also sure that she won't say no; because come on, you've saved her life before!"

"And you're the cutest princess I can ever imagine." He hugged me tightly, "Good night, little sis."

I smiled and hugged him back. "Good night, big bro."

Chapter Six

"Good morning everyone!" I smiled as I sat down for breakfast. "Good morning." they all replied.

I listened to my dad carefully as he interestingly described the temple's rooms, gardens, and hallways to my mother. I decided I wanted to go there and explore it in the nearest chance I get.

So after I helped clear up breakfast, I asked my dad if I can go explore the temple. He allowed me to, but Mehmet and Kaya Alp (a warrior) had to be with me.

When I was just about to start moving out of the tribe, Ertuğrul came up to me. "Did you ask Halime yet?"

"I will speak to Halime right when you guys arrive at the temple, and then after that you will be the one in charge of asking my parents."

He agreed. So with everything planned, I started off towards the temple.

The first thing that I noticed when I entered the temple was the slaves. They were a lot! My brother freed them all and gave them some money, clothes and food to start their new lives.

I was getting off my horse, when a girl my age came up to me with a smile on her face. "Hello, I think that you're Sara."

Sara Hatun

"Hi. Yes I'm Sara. Who are you?"

"I am Alexandra, a Byzantium girl. Your brother freed me from slavery, so I wanted to thank him. And I thought that I should meet you, because you seem like a nice person." She stuck her hand out for a handshake.

I gave her a handshake and replied "Nice to meet you Alexandra. We haven't done anything by freeing you and your friends from slavery, because our religion forbids slavery."

"But we are all Christians, so why do you guys care about us?"

"My dear sister, just because your religion differs from ours, that doesn't give us the right to not free you from the wild oppressors. For our prophet has said "god will not help or be by any unfair country's side, even if it was an Islamic country. But god will give victory to a fair country and be by its side, even if it wasn't an Islamic country."

"Thank you a lot! I will never forget your kindness." Alexandra beamed and went off to her friends.

**

When I entered the temple's main room, Sungurtekin and Gündoğdu were fighting. I ran up to them and stood between them. "Stop fighting! What are you guys doing? My dad put you guys in charge of the temple because he thought that you guys were mature enough! Turns out you're not!" I shouted at them to stop.

"Shut up Sara, no one asked for your opinion!" Sungurtekin said.

"It is nowhere near my fault that you guys are fighting like two little kids." I said back in an angry and really mad voice.

Just then my family entered the room.

Ayah Hamad

I was shocked; I thought that they were going to come in the afternoon!

"What is happening here?" my dad shouted.

We all just froze there for a second. Gündoğdu broke the silence with "Nothing dad, everything is all right."

Sungurtekin and I nodded.

My dad was obviously not convinced. He gave us a dark look as he sat down on the throne. Next he called us over and ordered the rest to leave the room.

I could tell that he was really mad. I wasn't surprised because my dad hated it more than anything when we fought. Every single fight among us led us to huge consequences.

"Can I know what happened here? Gündoğdu, you go first." My dad asked.

Gündoğdu answered: "Dad it isn't anything serious, but basically Sungurtekin and I were fighting…"

"About what?" my dad interrupted.

He paused, looked at Sungurtekin and then replied: "Sungurtekin killed a temple guard that quit and said he didn't want war…"

"And?" my dad asked.

"Isn't it not allowed in our religion? Like I mean if he wants to start a new page and all?" Gündoğdu perplexed.

"My son, our religion said that if a person who started war against you and then quitted gets killed except if he entered Islam! Yes, it won't be wrong if you helped any oppressed person. But you don't forgive anyone

Sara Hatun

that easily because I'm sure that that guard was just scared of death." dad replied.

Sungurtekin gave Gündoğdu an "I told you" look.

"And then what happened?" my dad questioned.

"Sara saw us fighting and tried stopping us, but she did it in a rude way, and then you guys came." Gündoğdu continued.

"Is that true Sara?" my dad asked turning towards me.

"Yes."

"You three know what you have to do now." Dad gently intoned.

So the apologizing session started. I watched as Gündoğdu hugged Sungurtekin and apologized.

When they finally finished, I apologized to both of them and set off.

**

I bumped into Halime in the hallway, so I asked her if she would like to go explore the place with me.

"I was gonna explore the garden just now. How about you join me?" Halime smiled.

"Sure!"

After minutes of just walking around the beautiful garden (it was so beautiful!) I broke the silence "did you ever think of marriage Halime?"

She paused for a while and then replied "Yes. I have always thought of having a man by my side after my dad died."

Ayah Hamad

"Do you have a particular guy in your mind though?"

"No."

"Would you want anyone from the tribe?"

"Doesn't matter where he's from. As long as he's just right, I'll be more than happy to spend the rest of my life with him."

"Oh."

"You seem like you have someone in mind."

I stopped walking and looked her in the eye. "What do you think of my brother Ertuğrul?"

"Oh!" her cheeks turned to a cute shade of pink. "He's a brave warrior and a handsome guy."

I started walking again, and I was so happy. "Would you marry him?"

Halime froze in her place, with a surprised expression on her face. So I held her hands and smiled "if you don't want to, no one will force you to. This is up to you."

"No, no, not at all. That's not what I meant. I would actually love to marry him; for he is the guy my dad would've wanted me to marry. I remember his words before the devils caught us."

She paused and sat down on a nearby bench. "He said that the right guy should be strong with a good heart. He wanted me to get married so badly. Because he said that he'll relax then. You know, he meant that if anything happened to him, he wouldn't worry for me because a strong man would be by my side."

Sara Hatun

I hugged her tightly and comforted her. "I'm sure that if your dad was here, he would've been very happy if you got married to someone you love and have faith in. A strong and brave man that is willing to do anything for you."

"True." She sniffled. "But will Ertuğrul marry me?"

"He would love to!" I smiled. "I have done my part now, Halime. Now both of you guys have to talk to each other and then discuss the matter with my parents!"

Chapter Seven

The next afternoon dad wanted a big feast done as in celebration for capturing the temple.

So mom called us all over to help her in the kitchen. This feast was going to be done in the temple and a later one was going to be done in the tribe, but the one in the tribe was going to be done for my dad, brothers and the tribal masters.

Everything in the kitchen was boring; I wasn't really into cooking. Mom saw how bored I was so she suggested "go supervise the women and help them. I guess it's better than being stuck on one thing."

So I started walking around the kitchen observing at all of the women work with the food. They actually seemed to enjoy it! After a while I realized that Halime wasn't in the kitchen, even though she was in here when I came in.

I asked mom where she was, and mom said that she was tired so she went to sit in the garden. I doubt it though, I'm sure that she is speaking to Ertuğrul. She informed me in the morning that she would speak with him this afternoon.

After we finished from cooking and preparing the dinner, my family met in the dining room. We sat down and started serving ourselves.

Sara Hatun

I loved the unification of my family more than anything; for it was amazing sitting around one table, eating together and joking around.

After quite a while of joking and talking together my dad started "my dear family, I want to discuss with you guys an important decision I have made. As you guys all know, the temple we are now in would be a thank you gift from us to the king of Aleppo. I have decided that after we give it over to Aleppo's king, we should all head back to Anatolia!"

"That's a great idea dear, but what about the Mongols?" mommy asked.

"More than half of the Mongols have gone to other parts of this world. I'm sure that we would be able to control the rest." My dad replied.

"Why didn't you tell us before dad?" I asked.

"I wasn't sure if everything was going to work out, so I have decided to keep it for myself, and now I've told you because I'm sure of my decision." daddy answered.

"Who is going to Aleppo's king to sort everything out?" Ertuğrul questioned.

"The king's palace is in our way to Anatolia. He obviously had to have heard of our victory, so I myself would go and thank him and hand over our gift." dad smiled.

Everybody started eating again except for me; because I was already full.

When everyone finally finished eating, Gündoğdu, Sungurtekin, Dündar and Ertuğrul got up to leave.

But dad stopped Ertuğrul and told him to sit down, because he had to discuss something important with him. So we all started getting out to leave them alone, but daddy surprisingly called me over too.

Ayah Hamad

When Ertuğrul and I sat down after the room got empty, dad started "you guys know how old I am; for barely anything is left for me in this world."

I held my dad's hands and sighed "dad, you know that I hate it more than anything when you speak like this!"

"God bless you." Ertuğrul added.

"Amen."

"I have a commandment before I die, that has to do with the both of you." dad stated.

He paused for a while and then continued "Sara, you aren't married yet, so you don't have a man to protect you and always be by your side. So because of that, after I die, I want you to always be with Ertuğrul. Treat him like you treat me now; respect I'm and listen to him. Same thing for you Ertuğrul, I trust you because I know that you are the closest one of her brothers to her."

"Your command dad, it will be my pleasure!" Ertuğrul smiled.

"Same thing here dad." I nodded. "But don't mention this again please."

"Alright! Thank you guys, now I can relax." Dad beamed.

"Estagfirullah!" Ertuğrul gently intoned. "Dad, I want to discuss with you and mom something important, if you have the time."

He gave me a wink, which meant that he wanted to discuss the marriage decision. Dad asked me to go call mom, so I hugged him (I freak out every time he mentions his 'nearby death') and left the room.

Mom was in the garden with Sungurtekin and Hateja, and I could tell from the huge smile splattered on her face that she was so happy.

Sara Hatun

"What happened mom? You look like you're on your way to paradise!" I curiously asked.

Mom pointed at Hateja and then Sungurtekin gushed "Hateja is pregnant! I'm finally going to become a father!"

"Mashallah Hateja!" I hugged her hard, but not hard enough to hurt her stomach.

"Congratulations Sungurtekin!" I effused and hugged him hard. I was so happy for him, because he had always wanted to become a father.

"Did you tell dad yet?" I asked.

"We just knew. Where is he though?" Hateja asked.

"Oh yeah! Dad and Ertuğrul are discussing something, and they want you to join mom."

"Okay, bye then!" mom said and hurried off.

"Bye!" we called after her.

I smiled at the rest and went off alone. My headache was still there, so I headed to my room for a nap. The room that I chose was huge and had two windows.

Through one window you can view the beautiful colorful garden and through the other window you can view the place (it was a small garden that contained tables and chairs) where some meetings are held. Halime's room was on my room's right side and my parents on the left side

**

I woke up from my nap just in time to pray Asr. I was still tired, and my headache was still there, but I decided to pray and then go for a walk.

Ayah Hamad

The walk will help me relax, and probably make my awful headache go away.

When I was in the hallway, I bumped into Mehmet. "Hi!" he greeted.

"Hey."

"Where are you going?"

"I want to go for a walk; the weather is really nice."

"Inside, to explore the temple's shops and gardens, or outside to explore the huge fields?"

"Inside." I paused for a while. "I would love to see how the traders and families are doing."

"Nice! Can I join?"

"Sure!"

The walk was quite nice. I enjoyed talking and introducing myself to the traders and families. They were very kind and sweet. After a while, Mehmet stopped to look at some cool knives and swords, when Alexandra came up to us. "Oh, hi!" I smiled.

"Hey. What brings you here?" she asked.

"Walking around. Thought it would be nice to know the people here."

"The people here are amazing and gorgeous. I love how they come from all around the whole world and meet in one place!"

"Yeah, true!"

Sara Hatun

"Oh yeah! I was thinking about something. The surroundings here are really nice. Why don't you come with me to explore outside the temple. We can get to know the area and each other more!"

"Sounds like a good idea. I'll ask my brother and be right back!"

"No, no! There's no need for permission; it's a really safe area!" she stopped me.

I gave her a suspicious look but decided to go at the end. I had a feeling that I will regret it; but we got rid of our enemies that are here anyways.

"Mehmet, you can go. We'll come back shortly."

We decided to go by foot since Alexandra didn't own a horse yet. But she was right! The nature around the temple was more than amazing!

We walked for a long time between green trees, through flower fields and small ponds. At the end of a long flower maze, we reached a steam and decided to stop for a break. I drank from the steam's fresh and cold water, washed my face and sat down. Alexandra came and sat down beside me.

We opened a random conversation about our families, when suddenly ten temple guards appeared from the bushes. As I got up the ten guards surrounded us. "What's happening?" I sputtered.

I started running away, but Alexandra grabbed my hand "not that fast!" And then she placed her dagger on my neck!

"You betrayer!" I spat at her. I easily ducked and grabbed the knife out of her hand (she was so weak). I then stabbed her on her stomach.

I was about to kill her, but one of the guards pulled me away. He tied my hands with a thick piece of rope, and started pulling me to somewhere while the others followed.

43

Ayah Hamad

I glimpsed from the corner of my eye two guards helping Alexandra get up to her feet and walk. I just don't get why she betrayed me. *She most probably did it for gold. She's so cheap. Betraying people who helped her for some rotten potatoes who bought her with gold.*

"What do you guys want from me? Leave me alone you witchy beasts!" I screamed.

"We will swap you with Halime; we need her for our plans against the Seljuk country. I'm sure that your family likes you more than they like her. You and your stupid family thought that you can end us up by capturing one of our many temples! I'm sure that before you would even guys have the chance to end five percent of us, we would have ended you people ages ago! The war just started." one guard snickered.

"Yes, of course it just did!" I agreed with a smug smile on my face. "But I'm sure that the results that you predicted will happen aren't true. Even mental people won't conclude that!"

After a while we had to stop because Alexandra couldn't walk anymore. I watched as a guard cleaned the stab and then bandaged it. She was giving me dirty looks but I ignored her. *No wonder Gündoğdu warned me about going out without informing him.*

He was going to get really mad; this is the second time I repeat the same mistake. I'm so dumb; my dad had always warned me about trusting anyone.

After a really long while a guard came and pulled me up. "Come on, we have to go!"

"Yes we have to go. Probably this will be the end, who knows?!" I spat at him.

Sara Hatun

"Shut up! No one even knows that you're with us; because no one really cares about you!" just as the words came out of his mouth an arrow was shot right through his neck.

"Whoa!" I yelped as I jumped out of the way. Seconds later Gündoğdu appeared with Mehmet and they started fighting the guards. I quickly took a sword that belonged to one of the dead guards from the floor, cut off the ropes on my hand and got into action.

I helped finish up the guards and at the end only Alexandra was left. I went up to her but Mehmet stopped me. "We need her for information."

I paused and then looked at my brother. (He was really mad!) "Come here Sara!" Gündoğdu instructed harshly. "Can you repeat what I have told and warned you about yesterday?" he asked after I went up to him.

"Not to go out of the temple's main gate before I ask for permission." I replied guiltily.

"And you?! What did you do?"

"Ummm…" I paused and looked up at him. He looked back and then (it all seemed to happen in slow motion) he… slapped me!

I felt my head go dizzy but my brother held me straight up. "If Mehmet wasn't there with you, god only knows what would have happened to you! I do this because I care about you Sara!" he scolded.

Yeah, of course it was Mehmet! I shot him a 'thank you' look and then I looked back at the ground. "Gündoğdu…" I started. "You're right in every word you have said. I know that you care about me and I've acted stupidly. I'm really sorry."

After a moment of silence he held my hands and gave me a sweet hug. I hugged him back really hard and felt some tears form in the corner of my eye.

45

Ayah Hamad

Gündoğdu noticed and wiped them off with his soft hands. "What really matters is that you're okay!" he comforted. "No betrayer stays without punishment!" he continued as we glared at Alexandra.

I convinced Gündoğdu not to inform anyone about the incident because I didn't want Halime to feel bad. She was such a sweet girl and I didn't want her to get harmed in any way.

Dad opened the 'Aleppo's King' conversation on dinner. "Did you boys plan anything?" he asked my brothers.

"Yes dad, we thought that it would be best if Ertuğrul and Gündoğdu go, while Dündar and I stay here and help you prepare for the tribe's journey." Sungurtekin began. "After Ertuğrul and Gündoğdu come back, the tribe will start off for the long journey. However, when we're near the king's palace, you and I will visit the king and thank him for everything."

"Excellent plan. When will you guys go exactly though?" dad asked Gündoğdu.

"We were thinking of tonight, if it's okay with you of course." He replied.

"Okay then. We will start preparing for the journey today." dad said.

"What about me? It's totally unfair if I get to do nothing!" I sighed.

Dad smiled "what do you want to do?"

"What about she comes with us to the palace?" Ertuğrul suggested.

"YES!" I excitedly asked. "Please?!"

"She should come with us dad! She will get to explore the palace and have the chance to learn lots of things!" Gündoğdu added hopefully.

"I can't refuse if that's what you all want!" my dad smiled. "But mommy has to be okay with it too."

"Thanks so much dad!" I smiled. "Mom, can I go? Please?"

"Of course sweetheart. But you have to take good care of yourself and listen to your brothers." Mom replied.

"Thank you!" I gushed.

"Yeah thanks dad and mom! I can finally have a break from Sara!" Dündar joked. I glared at him while the others laughed.

"Oh yeah!" my dad suddenly exclaimed. "There is something important to be done before we head off to Anatolia!"

"What is to be done dad?" Dündar curiously asked.

My mom pointed at Halime and Ertuğrul while my dad concluded: "A wedding!"

Everyone started cheering while Halime blushed. I squeezed Halime's hand and congratulated her. I was so happy! Everything was going on just fine, and I hope that it will stay like that. It was honestly a precious moment. A wedding always means happiness, and I hoped that it would be that way.

**

After dinner, the time arrived for my dad to speak to the families of the temple. As we all gathered around him, I realized that half of the people were scared, a fourth normally okay and the last fourth quite okay.

"Assalamu alaikum my dear brothers, sisters and kids!" my dad began. "I am Suleyman shah, the master of the kayi tribe. I would like to begin

Ayah Hamad

with a statement. All of you people here are free to do whatever you want; no one is to be harmed!"

"So you… You guys aren't here to make us slaves, prisoners or whatever?" a teenager interrupted.

"Estagfirullah! My dear son, as I have said, our point is to make people all around the world live in fairness, peace and love. For that's what our blessed religion teaches us to do."

He turned to the crowd and then continued "everyone here is free to do what they want; excluding harming anyone or anything of course. You are allowed to complete all of your religion practices, your daily life and so on. If anyone has something to tell me, you are to be welcomed at any time!"

"You mean we are free to do any of our religion practices?" an old woman asked.

"Of course!" dad smiled. "We won't harm or judge you because of your different religion."

"God bless you!" the crowd resounded. They loved my dad already.

It felt really good to be surrounded by happy and kind people.

'Oh Allah, allow happiness to surround us, making us forget what made us cry and what made us sad.' Amen.

Chapter Eight

I hugged my parents and rest of my family goodbye. This was the first time that I'll actually stay away from the tribe for days.

Ten warriors were joining us. The palace wasn't really far from the tribe; we would definitely reach before Fajr in a while. That means we would most likely not stop in the way for breaks.

"In the name of Allah, and Praise be to Allah. Glory unto Him Who created this transportation, for us, though we were unable to create it on our own. And to our Lord we shall return. Come on, let's begin our journey!" Gündoğdu called out.

I loved the feeling of the wind as I raced on my horse between my brothers. It wasn't a cold night; but it wasn't warm either. It was just perfect. I smiled to my brothers and we started galloping off faster. I wonder how the palace was going to be. *Would it be like prison or like paradise? Were the people there friendly or mean? Were they fair or oppressors?* I guess that I'll find our when we reach the place. Inshallah this will be a safe journey!

**

Oh Allah, help us to uphold the truth against the tyrants; and prevent us from advocating injustice to gain the applause of the weak.

Ayah Hamad

Oh Allah, if you make us rich, do not deprive us from happiness. If you grant us strength, do not take away our mental faculties. If you make us successful, do not deprive us of modesty. If you make us modest, do not deprive us of our pride and dignity.

Oh Allah, teach us to love others as much as we love ourselves. Teach us to judge ourselves, before we judge others. Teach us that tolerance is the greatest strength, and that vengeance is the first sign of weakness.

Oh Allah, if you grant us success, do not blind us by vanity. Do not make us despair if we fail. Please always make us remember that failure precedes success.

Oh Allah, if you deprive us of our wealth, do not let us despair. If you take away our success, give us the strength to overcome failure. If you deprive us of good health, do not deprive us of faith.

Oh Allah, if we hurt others, give us the strength to apologize. If people hurt us, give us the strength to forgive. If we are oblivious to thee, don't deprive us of your forgiveness and patience.

For you are all-powerful, all-merciful and all-capable.

Amen.

**

Gündoğdu (the leader) stopped us for a break.

I asked him why, since we were close to the palace. He replied with: "It will be better if we enter the palace freshened up, rather than entering it tired and hungry."

"How far are we from the palace?" I asked.

"We are really close. If you go up that hill, you will be able to see it."

Sara Hatun

I ran up the hill (I was tired and my legs started aching), but I finally made it to the top.

I was thrilled by the amazing view. The palace was surrounded by gardens of roses, flowers, trees, palm trees, streams and all sorts of cool things. I decided not to go down; but to stay in my place. I would easily sense when they wanted to go anyways from their voices and noises. After a while of viewing the gorgeous place, I heard footsteps. I quickly turned around but then realized that it was only Ertuğrul. I smiled at him as he sat down.

"Hey!" he said.

"Hi."

"Nice view, right?!"

"Yeah."

"You're sleepy."

"I am, but I don't feel like sleeping."

"Not like you have the time to do so, anyways."

"So we're leaving now?"

"Not this moment, but really soon."

"I bet that you're really excited to go back home!" I teased.

"Sure am!"

"So you're excited for the wedding, huh?!"

"Obviously. You were right. Halime is quite a nice girl."

Ayah Hamad

"When was I ever wrong?!" I smiled.

"Yeah sure, you were never wrong!" he laughed sarcastically.

"Hey! Ertuğrul and Sara! Come on down!" Gündoğdu called out from under. His voice was quite loud; but we could barely hear because he was far.

"Let's go!"

When we went down Gündoğdu had a beautiful dove in his hand. "What's up? I asked curiously.

"I think that if the king gets to know that we're arriving at his palace before he sees us, will be better than us surprising him."

I watched as the dove flew up and over the hill. They always said that doves stand for peace. I wonder how our trip was going to be. *Would it be peaceful or would it be hostile?*

We arrived to the huge palace in a short amount of time.

After the warriors off to their rooms (they had separate rooms in the ground floor), the king and his family greeted us in a really pretty room. Turns out he four kids:

- Mohammed; 20 years old.
- Walid; 18 years old.
- Amira; 19 years old.
- Yara; 16 years old.

His wife's name was Rima. They were all very kind.

"I'm very pleased to have you guys in my palace! Welcome!" the king started.

He then went off with all of the other males to a table in the corner. I gazed with admiration at my surroundings quietly until queen Rima came up to me.

"Hi Sara. Are you okay?"

"Hello, I'm okay. Thank you for asking though." I replied respectfully with a smile.

"Come on, sit down then!" she pointed at four chairs surrounding a table. I sat down in between Yara and Amira.

Tell us a bit about living in a tribe." Yara curiously asked.

"Life in the tribe is very different from life in the palace." I started. "In a tribe there are no walls surrounding you, and you totally feel free, while in the palace you're surrounded by walls. However, the tribe can be more dangerous, because there isn't much security."

"So you think life in a tribe is better?" Amira interrupted.

I haven't lived in a palace to judge…"

"Then how do you know what life is like in a palace then?" Amira asked.

"From a friend of mines." I answered. I meant Halime. She described the palace so much to me; it feels like I've lived in it before.

"Cool." Amira smiled.

"You can't say that life in the palace is better than life in the tribe. The palace and prison have no differences!" Yara sighed.

"I won't disagree. But if you have over protective brothers in a tribe…" I peeped at my brothers.

The queen laughed "girls, trust me... your families only want to protect you because they love you!"

"Yeah sure... more like torture us!" Yara rolled her eyes.

"Mom, in the morning tomorrow can I go out to the shops? Sara and Yara can join. I'm sure that Sara would love to explore this city!" Amira cajoled.

"If Sara wants to..." queen Rima said as she turned to me.

"I would love to!" I smiled.

"Take some warriors with you then." Rima said.

"See? Literally prison. People have to watch every single step you step!" Yara huffed. We all laughed; what she said was so true.

After we all finished eating (thy prepared a massive feast for us) and talking, Gündoğdu, Ertuğrul and I said our goodnights.

Then a servant led us to a huge room. The room was divided into three parts. I took the last part because it was the most private. After we all settled up, Gündoğdu called us over.

I asked him if I could go explore the shops in the morning. "You can go, but be careful. You don't know the city yet."

"Okay, okay!" I flatly said.

"When are we going to open the conversation about Anatolia?" Ertuğrul asked.

"Since the king invited us two to breakfast tomorrow, I was thinking of discussing it with him then." Gündoğdu replied.

Sara Hatun

"Okay." Ertuğrul yawned.

"So we're going to be headed back really soon, right?!" I questioned.

"I think so." Gündoğdu answered.

"Are you guys going to breakfast before we go explore the shops?" I asked.

"Yes. You won't even be awake by then." Ertuğrul replied.

"Right. Good night!" I could barely keep my eyes open.

"Good night." They both replied.

Chapter Nine

"Are you ready to go?" Amira asked as I approached her.

"Yeah. Where's Yara?"

Just as the words went out of my mouth she came running down the stairs. "Sorry, I've slept in."

"Let's just go. You always sleep in." Amira impatiently huffed.

"Stop acting like you're the boss here!" Yara growled.

"Shut up. I'm older than you, so respect yourself!" Amira sassed.

"Come on guys, let's go!" I sighed.

Just as we started moving forward, three guards crossed our way. "Stop right there!" one of the guards fired.

"How dare you!" Amira and Yara both stormed.

"I don't mean you two; I'm sorry. But we came to take Sara." The same guard said.

Sara Hatun

I gave him a surprised and confused look, and just when I was about to ask for the reason, Amira inquired "Why, what has she done?"

"She probably has nothing to do with this, but we are sure her brothers have." The second guard grimaced.

"Answer my question!" Amira commanded.

"Our dear king…" the guard began.

"WHAT HAPPENED TO MY DAD?!" Yara shrieked.

"He got poisoned while he was having breakfast with her brothers!" the guard glared at me.

We all gasped. I couldn't move. It's impossible for my brothers to have anything to do with this. I'm sure that whoever poisoned the king took advantage of our existence to throw all of the blame on us.

Yara fell onto the ground and started sobbing.

"And where is my father now?" Amira worriedly asked.

"He's in his room with the doctors."

Amira went over to Yara and lead her to her room. I could hear her sobbing "It's impossible for them to do this. Its, im…" she couldn't finish her words because of her loud sobs.

But I could tell that Yara and Amira were against the thoughts of us poisoning them, because they haven't shouted at me or gave me any bad looks. I just stood there- frozen in my place. "You guys are making a huge mistake…" I warned.

"Shut up! Denying things won't get you anywhere!" a guard clipped and harshly grabbed my arm. "Where are my brothers?!" I fretted.

Ayah Hamad

"In the palace's prison. They will stay there until the king gets up. Thanks god the poison wasn't that strong. Same for you- but you'll stay in your room." One of the guards informed me.

When we reached the room I shared with my brothers, he pushed me in and locked the door. I ran to Ertuğrul's bed, took his pillow and sank my head into it. I really wanted to see my brothers.

What are they doing now? Are they okay... or are they being tortured? I couldn't bare it. Being so close to them; yet really far from them.

I stomped to the door and started banging it very loudly. No one replied because no one cared.

When my hand started bleeding from how much I've banged it on the harsh door, I ran to Gündoğdu's bed.

I started having flashbacks to all of our memories. It was heartbreaking just thinking of them.

I finally felt myself drifting off to sleep, but the terrible night mares woke me up. *What if they actually killed them?* I couldn't stop worrying.

The next day, right after I prayed Asr, the queen stomped in to my room. I could see the despair, sadness and hate in her eyes. "We have given you a homeland, we have greeted you as true and actual friends and we treated you guys like you were part of our family. Yet this is how you treat us back. You poisoned the king! You killers!" she spat.

I just stared at the ground in silence because there was no way she would believe me if I tried to explain. The queen broke the awkward silence with "May god give you what you deserve and worse!" And with that, she stomped off with tears falling down her cheeks.

Sara Hatun

Next, I knew that there was only one thing that will help me and my brothers with this huge problem. I raised my hands to the sky and started making duaa deeply from my heart:

O Allah! I am your servant and the son of your servant. You hold me by my forelock. Your decree is what controls me, and your commands to me are just what I'm supposed to do. I beseech you by every one of your names, those which you use to refer to yourself, or have revealed in your book, or have taught to anyone of your creation, or have chosen to keep hidden with you in the unseen, to make the Qur'an Al-Karim the springtime of my heart, the light of my eyes, the departure of my grief, and the vanishing of my affliction and my sorrow.

O Allah! I seek refuge in you from distress, grief, incapacity, laziness, miserliness, cowardice, the burden of dept and from being overpowered from men.

Oh god, with your great powers and creations, I know that you're the only one that will help me get out of this massive problem. For my brothers and I have been oppressed; but not from our enemies, but from our dear friends. Ya Allah, you are the only one that have seen everything, and you are the only one that can solve everything. Please give the king the strength and power to get up once again with a healthy and strong status. Please god be by my brothers' side; keep them safe and good. You are our only hope in life! Oh god, if this is a test from you, please give us enough power to pass it and bless us with more patience. Amen.

**

After the duaa, I felt a lot better, because I knew that Allah swt was with us, watching every step that we step and every move that we move. I knew that Allah swt was going to help us, because our dear prophet Muhammad has said *"Beware of the supplication of the oppressed, for there is no barrier between him and Allah!"*

Ayah Hamad

The thing is that the palace assistants and guards weren't really mean to me. Like they didn't push me or swear at me, they treated me gently; but not too much. They obviously didn't want me to feel like I was okay and everything.

But my heart was aching; I couldn't bare stay away from my brothers for so long. Ugly and cruel thoughts just couldn't leave my brain and heart. *What if this…, and what if that…?!* Everyone obviously hated them like crazy now.

God protect them and keep them safe.

**

I woke up to an awful nightmare. I can't really remember what happened, but I do remember the main things. I clearly remember a red river (probably stands for blood) rushing by with a roaring sound; it was so creepy!

But the most thing that worried and scared me to death was the scene after the bloody river. It was my father's face fading away shouting for help! What if this was a sign to inform me something? I was so scared; I started shaking.

That's when I realized how much I miss my family and tribe. I really wanted to go back! But I guess that part of my destiny is to be stuck here.

It's already been two days; and there still was no news. The same things happen over and over again. The servants get me food; I sit there hopelessly sulking on the wall, wondering who would rescue us this time. And obviously I pray, make duaa and read Quran.

Just as I was thinking of all this, I hear a knock and then Yara rushes into the room. She scanned the room to check if anyone was there.

Sara Hatun

Next, she came and sat down next to me on my messy bed. "Sara, I know that you guys have nothing to do with this, and Amira also agrees. My mom is mad at you guys because I guess that she's in shock… but we will save you guys. I promise. My father will wake up very soon and he'll know the truth."

I smiled "Thanks a lot, Yara. I'll never forget your kind words!" I paused for a while and then asked "How are my brothers? They're okay… right?"

I let out a huge sigh of relief when she said that they were okay. Now my heart was more than relaxed. Alhamdulillah.

"And…" Yara paused and then continued "My dad is supposed to get up today. So by tomorrow I hope that I'll see you guys out again!"

"Inshallah."

At this very moment, I felt what the word 'relieved' meant. Tomorrow I'd most probably be on my way back to the great Kayi tribe. Well actually, if my brothers sorted everything out. If they didn't, we will have to stay for another day at least.

**

The next morning I woke up with a headache. I barely slept so I wasn't surprised.

But right when I decided to go back to sleep, a maid came in with my breakfast. I decided that I couldn't waste the food; so there was no sleeping time for me now. I guess that I'll just take a nap after Asr.

But something majestic happened when I was eating breakfast. When I cut the bread in half, a note slipped out of it! It read:

Ayah Hamad

I'm completely okay now. But I want to keep you and your brothers as prisoners; don't worry I know that you guys have nothing to do with this. This is a plan to catch the actual criminal. Thank you and have a nice day!

Sincerely, Ahmad, the king of Aleppo.

I was more than happy; for god has listened to my prayers through the seven skies! But I wondered how they were going to capture the criminal.

Amira and Yara answered my question when they came to visit me the next day. It turns out that the criminal dropped a note in the kitchen (so he was a staff member!) that read:

"Meet me in the shop near the huge mosque right after Maghreb and tell me what happened when you poisoned that idiot!" -SK

So the king is relying on the fact that the criminal thinks 'that the king believes we are the criminals.' So that way the criminal won't be scared and would lead his self to the prank.

The king his self and a small amount of soldiers (the whole note might be a prank –I hope not) would be waiting in the shop (but obviously they would be hidden). When both men arrive they will strike. Inshallah it will work! For just the thought of meeting my brothers was making me super-excited.

I guess that life in a palace can be very difficult. Waking everyday with the threat of death is a very scary and creepy feeling. But stories and morals always state that royals enjoy their lives without having any consequences. And now I totally get why these royals walk around with guards and security.

**

62

Sara Hatun

"Allahu Akbar, Allahu Akbar, Allahu Akbar...." the athan for Maghreb rose from the big mosque. I got up to pray but was interrupted by someone knocking very hard on my door. "Enter!" I sibilated.

But when who was banging on my door came in...

"Oh my god!" I chortled. I was so shocked and happy. "Gündoğdu?! Ertuğrul?!" I ran up to them and hugged them each so hard; I was so relieved.

"You guys are okay!" I beamed. "This is the most special gift that god could've ever gave me!"

"We're so happy to see you too darling!" Gündoğdu smiled.

"Yeah, we've been worried dead, thinking whether you're okay or not!" Ertuğrul added.

"If you guys were worried dead then how much do you think I was worried?" I sighed.

"Yeah, they always say that females are worry-guts!" Gündoğdu joked.

I laughed than questioned "what are you guys doing here if the criminal wasn't caught yet?"

"The king already left, and the criminal did too. So it wouldn't be dangerous if we went out." Ertuğrul answered.

"Yeah, that idiot won't know that there's a prank waiting for him!" Gündoğdu added.

"But what if the whole note was a prank?" I asked.

"You can't expect us to stay in prison for another weak!" Ertuğrul laughed.

Ayah Hamad

**

"So, did you guys sort out everything about us moving to Anatolia?" I asked as I handed my brothers their tea.

"Yes, we will return to the tribe tomorrow morning." Gündoğdu answered.

"Finally." I sighed.

"Isn't the king supposed to be back by now?" Ertuğrul asked Gündoğdu.

Right after Gündoğdu replied with "yes!" voices and noises rose from outside.

I ran to the huge window to check it out and saw the king on his way to the huge palace doors. As my brothers joined me, we saw the families of Aleppo greeting the king and swearing at the killer that was caught.

Him and his friend were tied up and were being pulled by two fierce-looking guys on horses. We couldn't tell who the criminal was, so we left the room and rushed down to greet the king.

When the king came into the palace and spotted my brothers and me, he hugged my brothers and nodded at me. "I am so sorry for what happened with you guys; for you guys were treated harshly. Our blessed prophet Muhammad has said *"Beware of injustice, for oppression will be darkness on the day of resurrection; and beware of stinginess because it doomed those who were before you. It incited them to shed blood and treat the unlawful as lawful."* I wish that you three forgive us all. Because I don't want anything to stay between us until the Day of Judgment!" he apologized.

"We are all the sons and daughters of Adam and Eve, and every human being makes mistakes. No one is perfect!" Ertuğrul replied.

Sara Hatun

"We are like a family, and we believe that forgiveness is the key to success. We all make mistakes." Gündoğdu added.

I nod in agreement and smile.

Just as the rest of the family members join, the queen apologizes to us and we reacted in the same way. She sounded like she was really mad at herself for blaming us. Especially when we knew who the real murderer was.

He was…

The king's personal cook! Unfortunately he was sent to the king's palace to earn the king's trust. His plan and the other people behind him was to kill the king. It was some kind of revenge they wanted. I think it was because the king killed the cook's father. The cook's father was a very bad person and the leader of a huge rebels group. God protect the king!

The next morning, when we were packing up to leave, the king came over to us. "I was very pleasured and pleased to have you guys in my palace. I hope that I can see you again after I see your father!" he lamented. "I wish that we spent a greater time together."

"Inshallah we will meet again, as long as Allah wants that to happen. We were pleasured to be at your palace too!" Gündoğdu smiled.

"We will leave you the temple as a gift from us. One day we will meet there!" Ertuğrul added.

"Inshallah!" I hoped.

Right after Dhuhr prayer, we set off to leave. It was painful saying good bye to everyone, especially Yara. But who knows, we might meet again!

Inshallah we reach the tribe without any difficulties.

Chapter Ten

After reaching the tribe, we had the wedding. It was more than amazing!

So first, everyone took their places in the partying tent. (It was a pretty and huge place, and fits the mood of a wedding. It was decorated with flowers and a whole bunch of other stuff.)

Ertuğrul and Halime sat down next to each other facing a sheikh. My parents were behind them, and Gündoğdu, Sungurtekin, Dündar, Hateja, Sude, Ali and I sat behind my parents. The tribal masters and our personal warriors sat behind us.

The sheikh started off by saying "La ilaha illa Allah, muḥammadun raslu Allah. There is no god but Allah, and Muhammad is the prophet of Allah." We all said it after him. "Princess Halime, the daughter of Mesud, do you accept to take Ertuğrul, the son of the Suleyman shah, the master of kayi tribe as your husband?" he questioned Halime.

"Yes." Halime blushed.

"Allah swt has said: *And give women their Mahr as a free gift, but if they of themselves be pleased to give up to you a portion of it, then eat it with enjoyment and with wholesome result.*" Do you agree on the dowry of 200 pieces of gold, to become the wife of Ertuğrul?"

Sara Hatun

"Yes." She answered.

"For the last time, do you agree?" the sheikh asked again.

"Yes!" she grinned.

The sheikh then turned to Ertuğrul. "Ertuğrul alp, the son of Suleyman shah, do accept to take Halime, the daughter of Mesud, as your wife?"

"Yes." Ertuğrul smiled.

"Do you agree to take her as your wife, considering the dowry that you promised?" the judge questioned.

"Yes."

"Do you agree?!" the sheikh asked.

"Yes!" Ertuğrul beamed.

The sheikh then turned to us. "Dear witnesses, do you witness?"

"Yes!" we all chortled.

Halime turned to face Ertuğrul and then said "I have given away myself in Nikah to you, on the agreed Mahr."

Ertuğrul beamed. "I have accepted the Nikah!"

Everyone cheered. "With the witnesses here and my witness, you two have become wife and husband. God bless you with happiness and amazing kids!" the sheikh confirmed happily.

"Inshallah!" we all said.

Ayah Hamad

After that everyone got up, and we all congratulated the couple. "May Allah bless for you Halime and bless you, and may he unite both of you in goodness!" my dad congratulated Ertuğrul.

"Amen!"

And with that, the partying started. It was so fun! We first had a meal and then a huge party outside. Everyone was cheering, dancing (men only) and joking around. At the end, Halime and Ertuğrul got into a horse carriage and went around the tribe. It was a magical marriage fit for a king and queen.

The next morning, it was the big day; we were finally moving to Anatolia!

"Right after breakfast, Sungurtekin and I will go to the palace. You guys also start moving after breakfast. Stop at the inn near the Euphrates River; for we will meet you there. I think that we will reach before you guys." my dad instructed at breakfast.

"Okay." mom replied.

"Gündoğdu, you will be in charge of everything while I'm gone." dad ordered.

"Your command dad!" Gündoğdu replied.

"You will be in charge of you siblings Ertuğrul!" dad turned to Ertuğrul.

"My pleasure dad!" Ertuğrul replied.

When we finally finished breakfast it was time for the journey. As my dad gathered the whole tribe (families, warriors etc.), he started *"Allah is the Most Great. Allah is the Most Great. Allah is the Most Great. Glory is to Him who has provided this for us though we could never have had it by our efforts. Surely, unto our Lord we are returning. O Allah, we ask you on this our journey for goodness and piety, and for works that are pleasing to you. O Allah, lighten this journey for us and make its distance easy for us. O Allah, You are our Companion on the road and the One in whose care we leave our family. O Allah, I seek refuge in You from this journey's hardships, and from the wicked sights in store and from finding our family and property in misfortune upon returning. We return repentant to our Lord, worshipping our Lord, and praising our Lord. My dear families and heroes, today we will return to our homeland as you know. This journey will lead us to the better Inshallah. Inshallah we won't face any difficulties on our way; may god lead us towards the best!"*

The crowd cheered; everyone was excited for the trip. After that my dad came over to my family "no one knows what will happen on this trip. But if anything happens to me…" he paused and we all sighed.

"Estagfirullah" I exclaimed. Dad smiled at me then turned to Gündoğdu "you will be in charge of the tribe. Take care of your family and the tribe; for they are what I leave for this world. Do your best to make them unique!"

"Estagfirullah dad! Inshallah nothing will happen to you!" Gündoğdu replied.

I sniffed and ran up to my dad. "You will stay with me forever dad!" I hugged him so hard as some tears fell down my face. I couldn't bare thinking about it.

Right after my dad and Sungurtekin hugged everyone good-bye and left; Mehmet came over to us running. "Sara, Sara!" he shouted. "Alexandra killed herself! She somehow found some poison!"

I gasped. "No way!" I stormed. "There has to be a betrayer in the tribe then! She can't have gotten that poison all by herself!" I was so mad.

"Calm down Sara! We're leaving anyways!" Ertuğrul tried to comfort me. I just stared at him blankly. He has no idea how important that

Ayah Hamad

beast is. I didn't have the opportunity to reply to him because Gündoğdu right away turned to order everyone to start moving. This was going to be a very long trip. I got up my horse and then Halime came up to me and asked whether I would like a race.

"Of course!" I laughed. There was nothing better than rushing past the wind through the open fields.

**

After a long while of us moving, (we had to go really slow because we were literally moving the whole tribe with us!) we reached Qal'at Ja'ber, a castle near the Euphrates. When we entered the palace we were greeted by Sungurtekin. He looked like the worst thing in his life ever happened to him. "Are you okay, my dear son? Where's your father?" mom asked.

A huge tear escaped his eyes. "Dad…"

"What happened to my dad?" I shouted.

Everyone stood there silently. "My dad… He…" Sungurtekin paused and then sobbed "He drowned in the Euphrates River when he was making Wudu for prayer."

The words hit me like a bolt of lightning. It felt like someone stabbed my heart with a dagger. I heard my mom screaming, and everyone else crying. Everything was blurry. I felt myself falling into a huge hole. I don't know what happened after that because I fainted. But the only thing I could remember was that awful nightmare I had in Aleppo. It was the most awful thing that could ever happen to me. Without dad, my life would literally look like a piece of trash thrown somewhere. No one would care about that piece of trash. I'm sure that I'll never get over this scourge.

**

Sara Hatun

I'm clueless of what happened after I fainted; but I woke up just in time for the funereal. It was more than awful; I couldn't even walk straight. Everyone was shouting and crying so hard; for everyone loved my father. It was unbelievable. *How can you lose a person that fast? He was my dad...*

He was my everything...

The worst part was burying him into his grave. The sand was stealing him from us.

I was sobbing so hard. When my brothers placed the last bits of sand on his grave, I ran up to his grave and stared in disbelief. It was awful. A daughter without a father is nothing. I was going to suffer. No male is going to love me the way he did.

I picked up some nearby flowers and placed them on his grave. *How would I leave him here and go off to Anatolia?*

Sungurtekin had to help me get up when everyone was lining up for praying on my dad's grave. Literally no one could hear the sheikh reciting from the amount of people crying.

After the prayer he started with the duaa *"O Allah, surely Suleyman shah son of Kaya alp is under your protection, and the rope of your security. So save him from the trial of the grave and from the punishment of the fire. You fulfill promises and grant rights, so forgive him and have mercy on him. Surely you are the most forgiving, most merciful. O Allah, forgive him and have mercy on him, and give him the strength and pardon him. Be generous to him and cause his entrance to be wide, and wash him with water and snow and hail. Cleanse him of his transgressions as white cloth is cleansed of stains. O Allah, enter him paradise and protect him from the grave and from the punishment of Hell-fire."*

Ayah Hamad

"Amen!" everyone sniffled. You could tell that the tone was so sad. My father was such a great person, god bless him with paradise.

I turned to observe my family members. Everyone was in shock; but you can't compare anyone's sadness with my mom. I went over to her and hugged her; it was so sad.

I used to be so close to my dad; we used to be perfect father and daughter.

And now he's gone.

I felt like I was going to be lonely in this world.

It was a total heart-break. There was no medicine for it.

But I knew that the most thing that could help him now is duaa.

**

We stayed in the castle until dinner. There was a huge dinner prepared for us but no one felt like eating.

Gündoğdu was now the master of the tribe; but it wasn't in a happy way. Like, obviously, there weren't any celebrations or anything. I felt bad for him because he had to deal with a lot of things. After no one ate dinner, he decided that it would be best to move to Anatolia.

So we start the journey again.

But it's not the same.

It's without my father.

Nothing will be the same now.

Sara Hatun

It will always get worse and worse; the farther and farther we are from his grave.

They always say that most problems heal with time. But I know that this problem won't.

Inshallah we reach Anatolia without any problems.

THE END

Printed in the United States
By Bookmasters